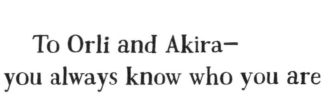

To Orli and Akira—
may you always know who you are

Published by Roaring Brook Press
Roaring Brook Press is a division of Holtzbrinck Publishing Holdings Limited Partnership
120 Broadway, New York, NY 10271 • mackids.com

Our books may be purchased in bulk for promotional, educational, or business use.
Please contact your local bookseller or the Macmillan Corporate and Premium Sales Department
at (800) 221-7945 ext. 5442 or by email at MacmillanSpecialMarkets@macmillan.com.

Library of Congress Cataloging-in-Publication Data is available.

First edition, 2022

The illustrations in this book were created in watercolor and typeset in Mrs Ant.
This book was edited by Connie Hsu and Mekisha Telfer, designed by Mercedes Padró,
and art directed by Jen Keenan and Aram Kim. The production editor was Jacqueline Hornberger,
and the production manager was Allene Cassagnol.

Printed in RR Donnelley Asia Printing Solutions Ltd.,
Dongguan City, Guangdong Province

ISBN 978-1-250-79836-7 (hardcover)
1 3 5 7 9 10 8 6 4 2

PINEAPPLE
PRINCESS

SABINA
HAHN

ROARING BROOK PRESS

NEW YORK

I am deeply, deeply misunderstood.

I know I am a princess,

but nobody believes me.

Princesses should do
whatever they want.

Especially at bedtime.

What I really need . . . is a crown.

I get to work.

With the law on my side and a crown on
my head, I shall be known far and wide
as the Pineapple Princess.

Am I sticky?

Yes.

Does my tummy feel funny?

Yes.

Am I very important?

YES!

My first subject has arrived.

More quickly follow.

We have picnics

and concerts

and royal hunts.

I am legendary!
I am **unstoppable!**

I am the
Pineapple Princess!

But there are problems.

My subjects are so demanding!
They never stop whining and
do not speak clearly.

They make poor soldiers,

worse cooks,

and terrible handmaidens.

I try to be a kind and compassionate ruler.
But it doesn't work.

So I imprison some.

And execute others.

I sense a rebellion.

I never wanted to be a princess anyway.

I am a
warrior queen!

My queendom for a horse!